Goes to Camp

For Stevie—J. N.
To Deborah—you've really grown on me—D. C.

SIMON & SCHUSTER BOOKS FOR YOUNG READERS

An imprint of Simon & Schuster Children's Publishing Division

1230 Avenue of the Americas, New York, New York 10020

Text copyright © 2006 by Jerdine Nolen

Illustrations copyright © 2006 by David Catrow

SIMON & SCHUSTER BOOKS FOR YOUNG READERS is a trademark of Simon & Schuster, Inc.

Book design and hand-lettering by Lucy Ruth Cummins

The text for this book is set in ITC American Typewriter.

The illustrations for this book are rendered in watercolor and pencil.

Manufactured in the United States of America

2 4 6 8 10 9 7 5 3 1

Library of Congress Cataloging-in-Publication Data

Nolen, Jerdine.

Plantzilla goes to camp / Jerdine Nolen ; illustrated by David Catrow.— 1st ed.

p. cm.

"A Paula Wiseman book."

Summary: Through a series of letters a boy, his parents, and others discuss Camp Wannaleaveee, the camp bully, and
Plantzilla, who has been forbidden to come but misses his caretaker and arrives in time to become the camp hero.

ISBN-13: 978-0-689-86803-0

ISBN-10: 0-689-86803-0

[1. Camps—Fiction. 2. Bullies—Fiction. 3. Plants—Fiction. 4. Humorous stories.] I. Catrow, David, ill. II. Title.

PZ7.N723Pl 2005

[Fic]—dc22

2003025643

Goes to Camp

Jerdine Nolen

Illustrated by **David Catrow**

A Paula Wiseman Book
Simon & Schuster Books for Young Readers
New York   London   Toronto   Sydney

April 15

Dear Camper and Parent or Guardian,

I am happy to inform you that you have been accepted into our preferred Outdoor Discovery Program at Camp Wannaleaveee. We are planning a rewarding summer for you.

We here at Camp Wannaleaveee have one goal: outdoor fun with youth! We strive to spend as much time in the outdoors as possible, to make new friends, and, most of all, to have fun in our woodsy forests.

Please fill out the attached forms and mail them back to us with full payment as soon as possible. We hope your son/daughter will find their stay a beneficial, memorable, rewarding experience.

Sincerely,

Dale Hadley, Superintendent

Camp Wannaleaveee · High atop the Green Mountains

Looking forward to meeting you!
Mel, JoANN, and Mena Hadley
Counselors

April 17

Dear Diary,

Mother and Father say that I am finally old enough to go to the camp Father went to when he was my age. I do not want to go. I do not want to be away from Plantzilla for even one day. Camp is a whole month long. Plantzilla and I have been together every day since last year when my science teacher, Mr. Lester, allowed me to bring home the class plant for the summer. My family loved him so much, we finally adopted him. I wish Plantzilla could come with me. But Father says we have to follow the rules of Camp Wannaleaveee. Pets are not allowed. But Plantzilla is a plant, too. What do I do? I leave June 8.

Until next time,

M

75 WATT
BULB MAK

Flora Flora Bora-Bora
ISLAND RESORT

June 10

Dear Mr. and Mrs. Henry Henryson,

Congratulations, congratulations, and more congratulations! You've won an all-expense-paid vacation to the beautiful island resort of Flora Flora Bora-Bora!

Flora Flora Bora-Bora is the single most exotic island in the entire world. The legends, mysteries, and romance associated with the words "Flora Flora Bora-Bora" are world famous. This wonderful vacation place is within your reach.

Our office will be contacting you to make all of your free travel arrangements! Remember that this is a once-in-a-lifetime chance. You'll never forget it.

Martin Pronounski, Travel Consultant

Flora Flora Bora-Bora Island Resort

Bora-Bora, South Pacific

11 June

Dear Mr. and Mrs. Henryson,

I would be absolutely delighted to plant-sit and pet-sit for you. It would fit in rather nicely with my comings and goings and would not be a bother at all. Besides, it would be very pleasant to spend some quality time with Plantcilia again. I will keep them safe here with me.

Sincerely yours,

Samuel G. Lester

Grade 3, Strewbrick's Lane Elementary School

UP⬆   DOWN⬇

Bus driver, Nathaniel P. diCherico
June 12
Bus Report
Zippy Bus Lines

Dear Bob,
  I am requesting an early vacation.
Desperately in need.
Respectfully,

Nate P. diCherico

Nathaniel P. diCherico
Driver 57, Zippy Bus Lines 849

CAPACITY
470 PASSE

June 15
Dear Mother and Father,
   Camp is O.K. Things are fine. I sleep in the same bunk that Father slept in when he was here. I have to make friends with the boy I share the cabin with — Bulford Whipland. He says rules are for everyone <u>except</u> him. There is a lot of poison ivy and poison oak. And there are a lot of bees. Mosquitoes, too, but they are mostly by the lake. It is against the rules to go near the poison ivy or the lake without insect repellent or without the counselors, Mel or JoAnn or Mena.
   Tell Plantzilla I miss him more every day. Does he have enough postage stamps? If only he were here with me. I'd better go now. The counselors are coming to begin our nature hike.
   I love <u>everyone</u> there,
        Mortimer
   P.S. Send pictures. They are allowed.

June 16

Dear Mother and Father,

Things are O.K. So far I've found the sticks and vines that I need to make a hot plate, but I have to share them with Bulford. Next week we make candles out of beeswax—only if we can find a way not to disturb the bees too much. I am trying very hard to do everything in a friendly way with Bulford Whipland. But it is a lot of work. He is the youngest and the smallest in a family of big people. But here he's bigger than everybody else, including Mel and Mena. And that is bigger with a capital B I G. Camp would be LOTS more fun if Plantzilla were here.

I miss EVERYONE there a lot, but sometimes I can't help feeling Plantzilla is nearby.

Mortimer

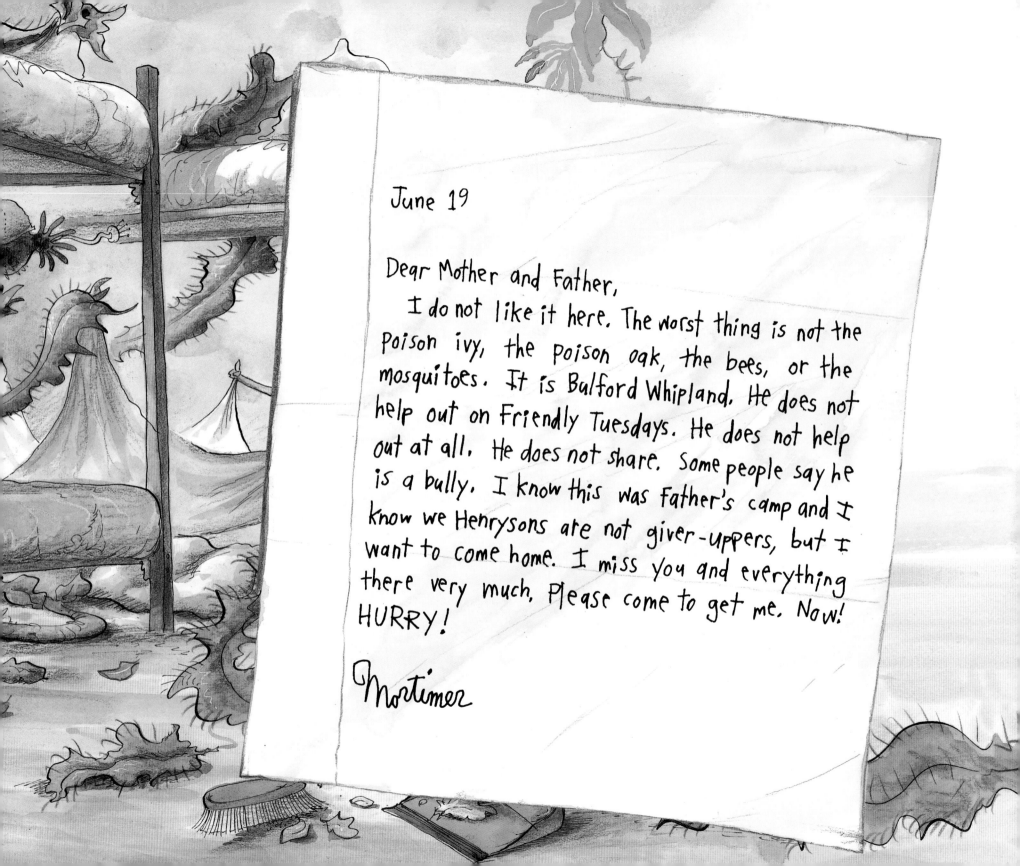

June 19

Dear Mother and Father,
   I do not like it here. The worst thing is not the poison ivy, the poison oak, the bees, or the mosquitoes. It is Bulford Whipland. He does not help out on Friendly Tuesdays. He does not help out at all. He does not share. Some people say he is a bully. I know this was Father's camp and I know we Henrysons are not giver-uppers, but I want to come home. I miss you and everything there very much. Please come to get me. Now! HURRY!

Mortimer

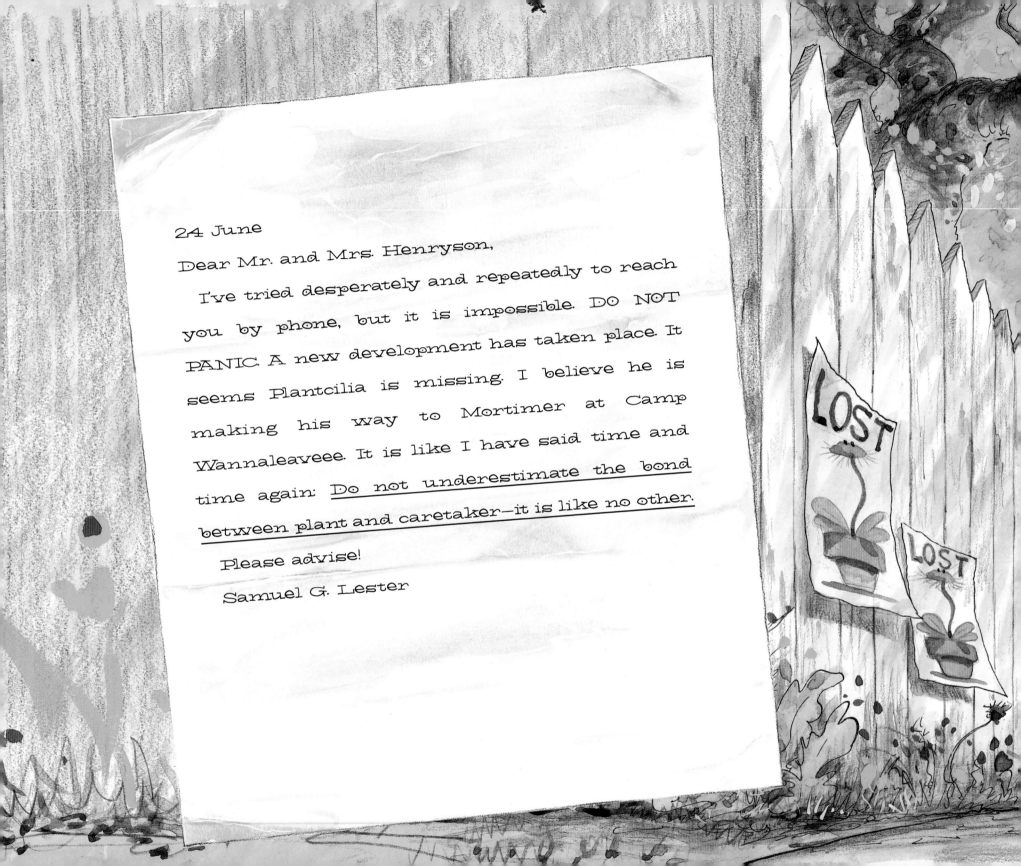

24 June

Dear Mr. and Mrs. Henryson,

I've tried desperately and repeatedly to reach you by phone, but it is impossible. DO NOT PANIC. A new development has taken place. It seems Plantcilia is missing. I believe he is making his way to Mortimer at Camp Wannaleaveee. It is like I have said time and time again: Do not underestimate the bond between plant and caretaker—it is like no other.

Please advise!

Samuel G. Lester

June 26

Dear Mother and Father,

I have the most wonderful news! Plantzilla is here with me at Camp Wannaleaveee!! He took the bus with Grollier. Plantzilla is _so_ amazing. He fits right in. Nobody ever has a worry with Plantzilla around. Don't worry about Grollier. Plantzilla and I will take good care of him, too. Plantzilla loves the mosquitoes. The bees are no problem for him either. They love his blossoms. We can go to the lake whenever we feel like it. As long as I stay away from Bulford, It is fun in the sun for me!

Write soon. Miss you.

Mortimer

P.S. Bulford Whipland is not very fond of plants or little dogs. Oops!

June 31

Dear Mother and Father,

The counselors weren't even upset when they found out Plantzilla was here. He saved the day. I heard Mel say, "Finally someone in the Whipland family was taught a valuable lesson he will never forget!" And Plantzilla was his teacher. Bulford learned a lot. He said being big does not give anyone the right to push others around. He could not push those bees around. You know, I think I could have stood up to Bulford all along. Plantzilla is the best, friendliest plant in the whole world. I think Bulford thinks so too now. He said he wants his family to meet Plantzilla. I'll see you on pick-up day next weekend. Please come early.

Mortimer

P.S. Remember when I told you that Bulford was a bully? He is very nice after all. We owe it all to Plantzilla. Bulford and I are going to be pen pals when we leave Camp Wannaleaveee. He may even come and visit us.

July 7
Dear Mr. Lester,
It is already the last day of camp and I'm sorry I haven't written sooner. It is just like you said, plants make all the difference in our lives. Life is perfect with Plantzilla around. And Camp Wannaleaveee is the best place for a pal like Plantzilla. Thanks for everything. See you in September.

Mortimer Henryson